This book belongs to:

My Arbor Day is:

To Emma—
May you grow up in a green and peaceful world.
And once again to Steve.
—K. O. G.

For each person who plants a tree for shady benches,
secret tree houses, swing-y tires, or maybe just nests and
treats—the world is just a little bit better because of you!
—C. M.

Published by
PEACHTREE PUBLISHERS
1700 Chattahoochee Avenue
Atlanta, Georgia 30318-2112
www.peachtree-online.com

Text © 2010 by Kathryn O. Galbraith
Illustrations © 2010 by Cyd Moore

First trade paperback edition published in 2015

Artwork created in watercolor and colored pencil
Title is hand lettered; text typeset in Goudy Infant

Printed and bound by RR Donnelley in July 2018 in Shenzhen, China

10 9 8 7 6 5 4 3 (hardcover)
10 9 8 7 6 (trade paperback)

HC ISBN: 978-1-56145-517-1
PB ISBN: 978-1-56145-922-3

Library of Congress Cataloging-in-Publication Data

Galbraith, Kathryn Osebold.
Arbor Day square / written by Kathryn Galbraith ;
illustrated by Cyd Moore.
p. cm.
Summary: In the mid-nineteenth century, as young Katie and her father help plant and
tend trees in their booming frontier town, she doubts that the spindly saplings will ever grow big.
Includes facts about Arbor Day.
ISBN 978-1-56145-517-1
[1. Arbor Day—Fiction. 2. Trees—Fiction. 3. Frontier and pioneer life—Fiction. 4. Fathers and
daughters—Fiction.] I. Moore, Cyd, ill. II. Title.
PZ7.G1303Arb 2010
[E]—dc22
2009017017

Arbor Day Square

Written by Kathryn O. Galbraith

Illustrated by Cyd Moore

PEACHTREE
ATLANTA

"Hmmm." Katie takes a deep breath.

"Everything smells new," she tells Papa.

And everything does.

Their prairie town is growing week by week. Now they have stores with glass windows. A church with a steeple. And a schoolhouse with desks for all seventeen students to sit in long rows.

Every week the train brings more
people who are eager for land.

The train also brings more lumber
and logs for houses, stables, fences,
and barns.

Papa helps pace out the town square.
It will be a gathering place for
concerts. And socials. And speeches.
Like the squares back East, the ones
back home, the ones they remember
as children.

Only one thing is missing. Katie
and the children know it. The
townsfolk and farmers know it too.

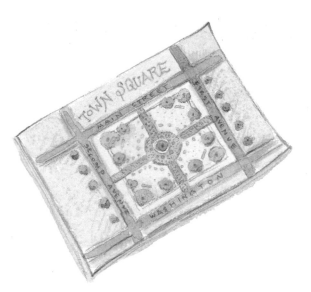

There are no trees on the prairie.
No trees for climbing.
Or for shade.
No trees for fruit or
warm winter fires.
No trees for birds. Or for beauty.

At the town meeting, everyone agrees that a proper town—their town—*needs* trees.

Mrs. Johanson passes a basket. Precious nickels, dimes, and quarters tumble in. *Jingle, jingle, clink.* Katie adds her own six pennies and Papa's silver dollar.

When the basket is heavy, Mr. Klein taps out an order over the telegraph lines.

SEND 15 TREES

Days tick by. Sunny days.
Rainy days. Windy days when
dust devils dance in the road.
At last the telegraph lines tap back:

TREES ARE COMING

TOOO-OOOOOOOOOOOO!

When the train pulls in, folks hurry
to the depot. Babies and dogs
come too. Katie skips beside Papa,
swinging her bucket and Dolly.

They're here!

Papa, Mr. Zimmerman, and all the O'Briens carefully unload the boxcar, counting as they go. "…thirteen, fourteen, fifteen!"

Katie stares at the saplings, spindly and green. "They're too little!"

"Don't worry. They'll grow," promises Papa.

But Katie isn't sure.

Katie and Papa follow the parade of trees to the new town square.

Papa and Mister Carter dig three holes.

Dig, swing, scoop.

Dig, swing, scoop.

Papa plants three small maples.

"Let me help," Katie says.
She gently pats the soil down
around each baby tree.

Under the warm sun, more trees spring up.

"Someday, these oaks will shade the bench," Papa says.
"And there, the elm tree will shelter the bandstand."

But Katie isn't sure.

Neighbors plant four maples near the church.
One apple tree on the corner.
And three chestnut trees in the dusty school yard.

Danny O'Brien leads the bucket brigade.
Katie lugs her bucket too.
Cool drinks for thirsty trees.
And dogs.

In a quiet corner of the Square, Papa and Katie dig a hole together.
Here they plant a flowering dogwood, in memory of Mama.

Katie touches the tender leaves. It is very little, but…

"Now this is *our* special tree," she whispers.

Papa hugs her. "Yes, our *very* special tree."

As the sun begins to set, the Square bristles and blooms
with green. Papa and Katie spread their blanket
next to Mama's tree.

Katie peeks into the basket.
There's plenty of food
to share with friends
and dogs.
And Dolly.

As old Doc fiddles up the moon,
neighbors gather their
children and dogs
and wave goodnight.

"Let's do this again next year."

And they do.
Year after year they gather in
the Square for another Arbor Day,
a tree planting day, a holiday.

Carrying shovels, rakes, and hoes,
Katie and Papa help plant trees
throughout the town.

Trees for climbing.
And for shade.
Trees for fruit and warm winter fires.
Trees for birds.
And for beauty.
And every year Papa laughs and
tells Katie, "Don't worry, honey.
They'll grow."

And every year they do.

It's another Arbor Day. Neighbors, kids, and dogs hurry to the Square.

Here come Katie and Danny O'Brien with their Megan Anne. Katie's papa—now a grandpa—holds one of Megan's hands.

In the Square lies a small row of saplings, spindly and green.

Katie smiles. "One day that willow will sweep the pond," she says. "And there, the cedar will sweep the sky."

Megan shakes her head and Katie laughs. "Don't worry, honey. They'll grow. Now, let's find your Grandma tree."

Megan runs across the Square. Her family follows just behind.

There Katie spreads out their blanket under the blooming dogwood tree. Robins rustle in the leaves. Sparrows chirp and flutter.

Megan peeks into the basket. There's plenty of food to share with friends, and dogs. And Bear.

When the moon rises, silver and round, neighbors gather up children and grandchildren and whistle for the dogs. "See you here again next year," they call.

And they do.

Celebrating
families,
trees,
and
neighbors.

Year after year.

And the year after that.

Author's Note

ARBOR DAY, founded by J. Sterling Morton, was first celebrated in the new state of Nebraska on April 10, 1872.

In 1854, the young journalist and his bride left the forested state of Michigan and moved to the plains of what was then called the Nebraska Territory. There, in Nebraska City, he soon became the editor of the territory's first newspaper. Later he devoted himself to politics.

In 1872, Morton proposed to the State Board of Agriculture that a day be set aside to plant trees. Morton encouraged his fellow citizens as well as civic organizations and schoolchildren to participate.

People were eager to join in. Trees were needed as building materials, as fuel to heat their homes, and as windbreaks for the new farms. They were also needed for their shade and their beauty. The day was a huge success. Over one million trees were planted throughout the state on that first Arbor Day.

Two years later, Governor Robert W. Furnas issued a proclamation asking the citizens to observe Arbor Day. In 1885, Arbor Day became a legal holiday in Nebraska.

Today Arbor Day is celebrated in all fifty states. The most common date is the last Friday in April, but it can vary from state to state, depending on the best planting time for the trees.

The idea of Arbor Day has spread beyond our borders and is also celebrated in many countries around the world, including Australia, New Zealand, Canada, Brazil, China, Germany, India, Mexico, and England.

If you would like to know more about the history of Arbor Day and the date it is celebrated in your state, please check the website of the National Arbor Day Foundation (*www.arborday.org*).